A Note to Parents and Teachers

Kids can imagine, kids can laugh and kids can learn to read with this exciting new series of first readers. Each book in the Kids Can Read series has been especially written, illustrated and designed for beginning readers. Humorous, easy-to-read stories, appealing characters and topics, and engaging illustrations make for books that kids will want to read over and over again.

To make selecting a book easy for kids, parents and teachers, the Kids Can Read series offers three levels based on different reading abilities:

Level 1: Kids Can Start to Read

Short stories, simple sentences, easy vocabulary, lots of repetition and visual clues for kids just beginning to read.

Level 2: Kids Can Read with Help

Longer stories, varied sentences, increased vocabulary, some repetition and visual clues for kids who have some reading skills, but may need a little help.

Level 3: Kids Can Read Alone

More challenging topics, more complex sentences, advanced vocabulary, language play, minimal repetition and visual clues for kids who are reading by themselves.

With the Kids Can Read series, kids can enter a new and exciting world of reading!

Sam Goes Next Door

Written by **Mary Labatt**

Illustrated by **Marisol Sarrazin**

Kids Can Press

Text © 2006 Mary Labatt
Illustrations © 2006 Marisol Sarrazin

Kids Can Press acknowledges the financial support of the Government of Ontario, through the Ontario Media Development Corporation's Ontario Book Initiative; the Ontario Arts Council; the Canada Council for the Arts; and the Government of Canada, through the BPIDP, for our publishing activity.

Published in Canada by
Kids Can Press Ltd.
29 Birch Avenue
Toronto, ON M4V 1E2

Published in the U.S. by
Kids Can Press Ltd.
2250 Military Road
Tonawanda, NY 14150

www.kidscanpress.com

Edited by Jennifer Stokes
Designed by Marie Bartholomew
Printed and bound in China

The hardcover edition of this book is smyth sewn casebound.
The paperback edition of this book is limp sewn with a drawn-on cover.

CM 06 0 9 8 7 6 5 4 3 2 1
CM PA 06 0 9 8 7 6 5 4 3 2 1

Library and Archives Canada Cataloguing in Publication

Labatt, Mary, [date]
   Sam goes next door / written by Mary Labatt ; illustrated by
Marisol Sarrazin.

(Kids Can read)
ISBN-13: 978-1-55337-878-5 (bound) ISBN-10: 1-55337-878-4 (bound)
ISBN-13: 978-1-55337-879-2 (pbk.) ISBN-10: 1-55337-879-2 (pbk.)

1. Dogs – Juvenile fiction. I. Sarrazin, Marisol, 1965–
II. Title. III. Series: Kids Can read (Toronto, Ont.)

PS8573.A135S2438 2006   jC813'.54   C2005-907048-X

Kids Can Press is a **l.orus**™ Entertainment company

Sam saw a big truck.

It stopped at the house next door.

Three movers jumped out.

They took things out of the truck.

"Hmm," thought Sam. "What is this?"

A sofa went into
the house.

A chair went into
the house.

A table went
into the house.

A car stopped beside the truck.

A family got out.

There was a mother, a father,

a little boy and a little girl.

"This is good," thought Sam.

"The new family has kids.

I like kids."

Joan and Bob took Sam to the backyard.

Sam peeked through the fence.

"Wow!" she thought.

"The kids have toys and food!"

"Woof!" said Sam.

She wagged her tail.

"Woof! Woof!"

9

The little girl saw Sam.

"Look!" she cried.

"A puppy!

Come and play, puppy!"

Sam ran to Joan and Bob.

She ran back to the fence.

"Woof!" she said.

"Woof! Woof!"

Joan laughed.

"You can't go next door, Sam," she said

"They are busy!"

Joan took Sam inside.

Sam flopped down.

"I want to play," she thought.

"I want to play with the kids."

The doorbell rang.

Joan went to the door.

It was the kids!

"Can the puppy play?" asked the girl.

"Yahoo!" thought Sam.

She jumped in little circles.

"I can play with the kids!"

Sam went next door with the kids.

"Let's play a game," said the little girl.

"I love games!" thought Sam.

"Puppies are good at games!"

"We are going to play family,"

said the little girl.

"Yuck," thought Sam.

"This is NOT a good game for puppies!"

"You are the baby," said the little girl.

She put Sam in the baby buggy.

"Now the baby will eat," said the little girl.

"Good," thought Sam.

"I like to eat."

"Here, baby," said the little girl.

"Here is some cake,"

Sam chomped on the cake.

"Yuck!" she thought.

"This cake is made of plastic!"

"Here, baby," said the little boy.

"Here is a cookie."

Sam chomped on the cookie.

"Yuck!" she thought.

"This cookie is made of mud!"

"Here, baby," said the little girl.

"Here is a salad."

Sam chomped on the salad.

"Yuck!" she thought.

"This salad is made of grass!"

Sam jumped out of the baby buggy.

She ripped off the baby clothes.

"Grrr," said Sam.

"Bad baby!" cried the little girl.

"Bad baby!" cried the little boy.

"You are supposed to be the baby!"

"This baby game is NOT for puppies!"

thought Sam.

"I will show you games for puppies!"

"Woof!" said Sam.

She grabbed a toy and ran

The kids chased her.

Sam ran and ran.

"Woof!" said Sam.

She grabbed a blanket and pulled.

The kids pulled, too.

Sam growled and growled.

"Woof!" said Sam.

She went to the sandbox and dug.

The kids dug too.

Sam dug and dug.

"Puppies do not like to dress up,"

thought Sam.

"Puppies do not like plastic cake.

Puppies do not like mud cookies.

And puppies do not like grass salads!

I will show you what puppies like."

Sam growled.

She jumped around the kids.

She barked and barked.

She rolled in the mud.

She chewed the toys.

She ripped up the baby clothes.

"This is fun!" thought Sam.

"I know good games for puppies!"